ABOUT THE BOOK

Over the years of my swimming and coaching career, I have seen people get [so caught up in what others are] doing that they forget to pay attention to themselves! Sometimes young swim[mers don't] understand that the best way to improve is to use their energy and concentration thinking about themselves and how to do their best. After all, the only person whose outcome they can affect is their own!

My philosophy for improving as an athlete boils down to two words: pay attention! First, kids have to pay attention to their coach, so they know what they are supposed to do. Then, they have to pay attention to themselves to be sure that they are actually doing it! Once kids can master these two skills, you will see them soar. Of course, they will have to pay attention every day and practice using those skills correctly until doing them right becomes habit!

When kids know they have worked hard and done the right thing, they have the confidence to swim well. The goal of this book is to teach kids that it is the journey that counts, not the destination. Anyone who works hard, focuses on themselves and doing their best, and puts thought and effort into what they do every day will see great improvement. More importantly, they will be a champion, no matter where they finish in their race!

Elli

ABOUT THE AUTHOR

Author Elli Overton is a three-time Australian Olympian and mother of two beautiful boys. Elli was a World Short Course, Pan Pacific, Commonwealth Games, and Australian Champion, but an Olympic medal eluded her. Plagued by feelings of being a loser because she never won an Olympic medal, Elli hid from the world of swimming for 12 years after her retirement. Now Elli is back, her focus on coaching and teaching swimming. She is dedicated to helping others reach their potential and appreciate their success. Still striving to reach her own potential, Elli has finally learned to value and celebrate her own achievements, big and small.

ellivertontrainingsystems.com

ABOUT THE ILLUSTRATOR

Jonathan Horstmann is a freelance illustrator, videographer, musician, and dreamer living in Austin, Texas. When he isn't busy being a full time Gemini he runs a non-profit which connects communities through small scale shared agriculture.

For more information visit **foodisfreeproject.org.**

For my little Seals and for the coaches I have most loved, admired and learned from – Gary Winram, Mike Walker, and Teri McKeever. EO

For the children of the future. JH

Published by CreateSpace Independent Publishing Platform

Charleston, SC, USA

First American Paperback Edition

Text copyright © 2013 by Elli Overton

Illustrations copyright © 2013 by Jonathan Horstmann

Library of Congress Control Number: 2013908692

ISBN-13: 978-1484131954

ISBN-10: 1484131959

Design and layout by Hollie Meador, One Pulse Medium, onepulsemedium.com

JAY'S SWIMMING JOURNEY

How one little swimmer learned to pay attention to what's important!

WRITTEN BY ELLI OVERTON   ILLUSTRATED BY JONATHAN HORSTMANN

It's the first day of practice for the summer, and all the kids are waiting their turn to dive in. Except Chance. He cuts in front of the others.

Susie sees him push in front of her friend and tells him, *"Jay, Chance cutted you!"*

Jay isn't bothered.

He tells Susie, "Oh, I don't mind. Someone gets to go first, and someone gets to go last... It doesn't matter where you start from."

Jay is busy thinking about what the coach said and doesn't pay attention to what the other kids are doing around him.

He thinks to himself, "What did Coach say? Oh yeah, we are doing freestyle with big arms and breathing to the side. I can do that!"

Jay is using his eyes and ears to watch and listen. He knows it's important to pay attention when the coach is talking.

"You need to learn to swim your strokes properly so you don't get disqualified in a race. 'Disqualified' is when you don't follow the rules of the strokes, and your result doesn't count, even if you won your race," says Coach.

"I won my heat!"

Chance is proud that he came in first in his heat. There were lots of kids his age in other races too, so he goes to check the results sheet to see where he finished overall.

Chance feels confused that he won his race but got disqualified. That's why it's important to learn to swim properly and follow the rules of the strokes: so that your results count.

"Let's do it right in practice kids, so you do it right in the race!" says Coach.

At the meet Jay swims his own race as best he can.

Jay is thinking about the big swim meet coming up.

Jay says, "Next week is Champs, Dad! Are we really going to swim at that big pool at the University?"

"Yes, Son. It will be fun! Lots of Olympians have swum in that water. They say it is magic! Do you feel ready?" Dad asks.

"Yes! I haven't won any heat ribbons yet, but I have had so much fun, and now I know how to swim just right!" says Jay.

Being at a big swim meet can make you feel nervous, but Jay feels confident because he knows he worked hard in practice.

"I sure am nervous! But I know how to do this. I did this everyday in practice. I just do the same thing here. I know I can do this well!" thinks Jay.

"He said he knows how to swim now—and he sure was right!" says Jay's dad.

Jay worked towards the results he wanted by paying attention every day. It feels so good to know that you did your best!

A Special Thank You to
Friends, Family and Supporters:

Hollie Meador, Layout and Graphic Design

Jessica Leonardo Doss, Editor

Circle C Seals Swim Team

Chrissie Jarrell

Clara Spriggs Adams

Kris Luck

Ned and Vivienne Overton

Mike and Tracy Koleber, Nitro Swimming

Kathy Overton and Lena Juross

The Eshuys Family, Bondi

Scott and Katie Schofield

The Lange Family, Darren Lange Swim Academy

Dave Holsey

The Beauchamp Family

40853052R00017

Made in the USA
Middletown, DE
24 February 2017